Clarence BLOOMS in Winter

Introducing Clarence, the Original Plantasaurus

Written by Adrienne Anbinder   Illustrated by Marian Pickman

AuthorHouse™
1663 Liberty Drive
Bloomington, IN 47403
www.authorhouse.com
Phone: 1-800-839-8640

© 1981, 2009 Adrienne Anbinder Illustrations by Marian Pickman. All rights reserved.

No part of this book may be reproduced, stored in a retrieval system, or transmitted by any means without the written permission of the author.

First published by AuthorHouse   5/26/2009

ISBN: 978-1-4389-7028-8 (sc)

Printed in the United States of America
Bloomington, Indiana

This book is printed on acid-free paper.

Clarence BLOOMS in Winter
Introducing Clarence, the Original Plantasaurus

Written by Adrienne Anbinder   Illustrated by Marian Pickman

Clarence was the only Plantasaurus in the whole wide world.

Clarence thought he was funny looking.

None of the others said, "You're funny looking," but he figured he must be because his nose seemed larger than all the other noses he had ever seen.

Clarence often hung his head when he walked so that the others couldn't get a good look at his nose.

He got to know his feet quite well because he never lifted his head all the way up. *They'll laugh at my nose*, he thought.

In the spring, when Clarence would look in the mirror, all that he would see was a large nose staring back at him. He didn't notice his buds opening fresh and fragrant, the yellow nodding daffodils, or the tiny new leaves unfolding to greet the day.

Clarence didn't notice much of anything but his nose. He didn't even notice the glowing faces of the others as they witnessed the incredible beauty of Clarence in the springtime.

What a sight Clarence was in the summer! Glorious pink roses, scarlet poppies, lilies of the valley, and brilliant blue morning glories stretched lazily down his back. Buzzing bumblebees and purple butterflies danced in celebration. And how wonderful Clarence smelled!

All of the others would stop and stare and point and marvel. But Clarence would just hang his head lower. He could not see how much beauty he brought into the world.

In the fall, all Clarence could see was how large his nose looked. He didn't notice the amber glow of colors that surrounded him,

or the red, yellow, and orange leaves that were brown and crumbly at the edges, or the shiny crabapples and purple grapes that hung from him, delicious and ripe.

Nor did he notice how the others beamed.

Then winter arrived, wild and white,

and Clarence was bare.

All of his rainbow colors were gone now.

The others no longer pointed at him, noticed him, or made a fuss over him at all.

"Why aren't they pointing at me?" He said to his mirror. "Did my nose shrink?" He stared a good long time. Finally, there was no doubt about it. Clarence convinced himself that his nose did, in fact, look smaller.

Little butterflies of joy began to tickle Clarence.
He felt quite pleased with himself.

Slowly, Clarence lifted his head high and proud. How warm the sun felt on his face. How clean and crisp the winter air felt in his lungs.

And for the first time during all of the seasons that came and went, Clarence smiled a deep, wide, genuine smile.

And the others saw.

One by one, little by little,

they all smiled back.

Clarence beamed, looking more radiant than ever.
The others were illuminated by his glow.

"How very lucky I am!" Clarence shouted with joy.

THE END

ABOUT THE AUTHOR

Adrienne Anbinder is the former owner of a New York greeting card company, and has owned her own Atlanta ad agency—along with her husband and partner—for nearly twenty years. She has written and art-directed hundreds of ads during her career in advertising. She has also raised two wonderful daughters. *Clarence Blooms In Winter* has been living for over 30 years in Adrienne's desk drawer. When she read it to her two grandsons, they were in awe. A chance meeting last winter with Marian, her original illustrator, sparked Clarence's rebirth.

ABOUT THE ILLUSTRATOR

Marian Pickman, mother of two grown daughters and grandmother of seven, has been a free-lance graphic designer for over 25 years. She has designed children's toys, children's furnishings, numerous logos, and greeting cards for companies such as Russ Berrie Inc. In addition, Marian regularly works on commissioned murals in New York City, where she currently resides. Her desire has always been to create an original children's book that would showcase her imaginative illustrations. Working with Adrienne on *Clarence Blooms in Winter* has been a dream come true. She looks forward to illustrating many more books for the Clarence series.